STORYTIME COLLECTION
STORYTIME COLLECTION

This book belongs to

_____

_____

Autumn
Publishing

Published in 2019
by Autumn Publishing
Cottage Farm
Sywell
NN6 0BJ
www.igloobooks.com

© 2019 Disney Enterprises, Inc.
Autumn is an imprint of Bonnier Books UK

1019 002.01
2 4 6 8 10 9 7 5 3
ISBN 978-1-78905-236-7

Printed and manufactured in China

Disney

Aladdin

Good evening, worthy friend. What I hold before you is no ordinary lamp. In fact, it once changed the course of a young man's life – a young man, who, like this lamp, was more than what he seemed – a diamond in the rough. Read on to discover a tale full of adventure and friendship. A story about how what's on the inside is the most important thing of all.

It all began one dark night, with an evil man continuing his quest for the ultimate power…

Deep in the Arabian Desert, an evil sorcerer called Jafar and a thief named Gazeem, stood outside the Cave of Wonders, the entrance to which was a giant tiger's head.

Too afraid to go into the cave himself, Jafar ordered Gazeem to go. As the thief moved nervously towards the entrance, the tiger boomed, "Only one may enter here – the Diamond in the Rough!"

Despite this warning, Gazeem hesitantly stepped inside. Suddenly, the tiger head entrance collapsed and the man disappeared under the sand!

Watching on, Jafar said, "I must find this Diamond in the Rough."

Early the next morning, in the market place of Agrabah, a poor street urchin named Aladdin took a loaf of bread without paying. "Stop, thief!" shouted a palace guard.

With no parents to care for him, Aladdin needed to steal to eat. He was also excellent at outsmarting the guards and quickly escaped their clutches.

Aladdin and his best friend, a monkey called Abu, lived on a rooftop in Agrabah from where they could see the Sultan's palace. Aladdin looked at it longingly. "Someday, Abu, things are going to change. We'll be rich, live in a palace and never have any problems at all."

At the palace, Princess Jasmine had a problem. Her father, the Sultan, said the law required her to marry by her next birthday – this was only three days away!

Her father had chosen several princes for her to choose from, yet Jasmine didn't like any of them. She wanted to marry for love, but her father simply didn't understand. To him, the law must be obeyed.

The Sultan, unsure what to do about his daughter, spoke to his most trusted advisor – Jafar. The sorcerer told the Sultan he could help, but would need the Sultan's Mystic Blue Diamond ring to do so. The Sultan was hesitant, so Jafar hypnotised him long enough to take the ring from him.

Now, Jafar could use the ring to find the Diamond in the Rough he so desperately needed.

While Jafar plotted and planned, Jasmine decided she would rather leave her life as a princess than be forced to marry against her will.

"I'm sorry, Rajah," she said to her faithful tiger. "But I can't stay here and have my life lived for me. I'll miss you."

So, with her tiger's help, the princess climbed over the palace wall and was gone.

The next morning, Jasmine walked through the marketplace, delighted by the sights and sounds. She noticed a young boy wanted an apple, so took one from the stall and gave it to him. Having spent her entire life away from the real world, Jasmine didn't realise she was stealing.

The stall owner wasn't very happy and confronted Jasmine. "Thief!" he shouted, as he took out his sword. Suddenly, Aladdin, who'd seen the whole thing, jumped in front of Jasmine and convinced the angry man that she wasn't a thief, just confused. The pair of them managed to walk away unharmed.

Meanwhile, in his secret chamber, Jafar used the Sultan's diamond ring to activate the Sands of Time. "Reveal to me the one who can enter the cave," Jafar commanded the magical hourglass. Suddenly, an image appeared inside the glass. "There he is… my Diamond in the Rough."

The sands inside were showing Aladdin! Jafar ordered the palace guards to bring the boy to the palace.

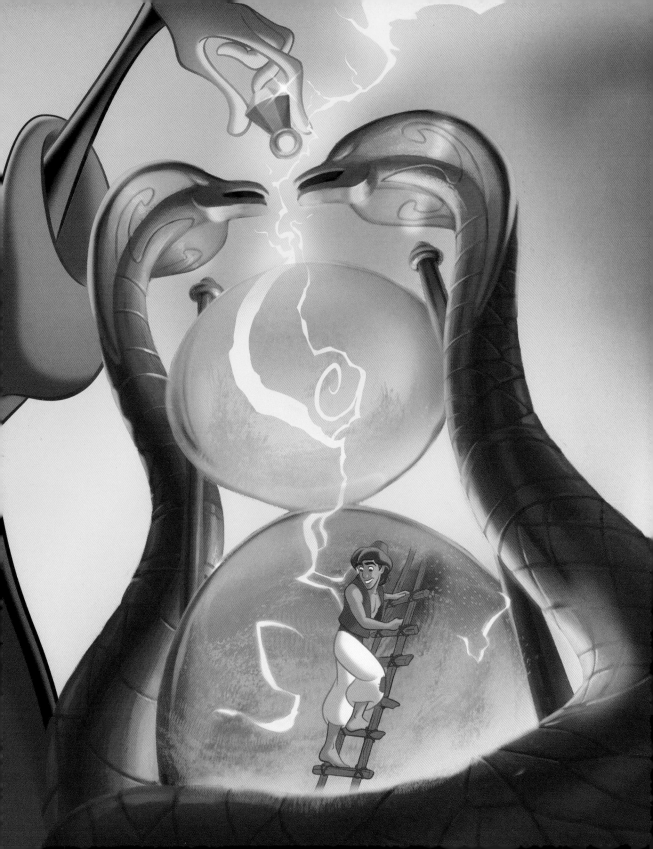

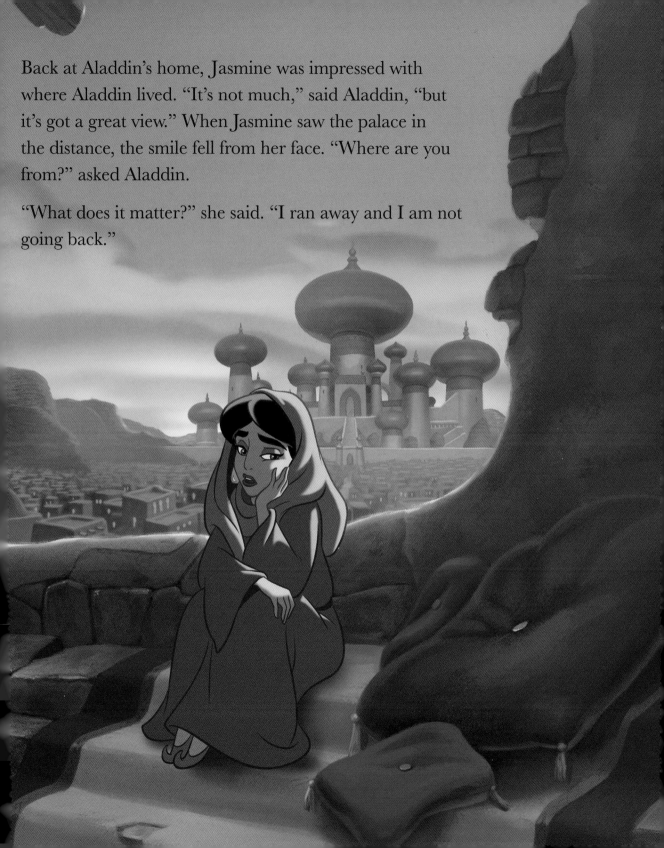

Back at Aladdin's home, Jasmine was impressed with where Aladdin lived. "It's not much," said Aladdin, "but it's got a great view." When Jasmine saw the palace in the distance, the smile fell from her face. "Where are you from?" asked Aladdin.

"What does it matter?" she said. "I ran away and I am not going back."

Suddenly, the palace guards
thundered up the stairs towards
Aladdin and Jasmine. "Here you
are!" shouted a guard.

"They're after me!" Jasmine and
Aladdin both cried together.

The guards were actually only after
Aladdin and they quickly caught him.
Jasmine threw off her scarf to reveal her
royal identity and asked them to release
Aladdin, but they refused.

The guards locked Aladdin and Abu in a deserted dungeon. Aladdin couldn't help feeling frustrated about Jasmine. She was a princess! No matter how much he liked her, he'd never see her again. He was a street rat and she deserved a prince.

Just then, an old man appeared. He offered to make Aladdin rich – rich enough to impress a princess – if the boy would do one small errand for him. When the old man opened a secret passage that led out of the dungeon, Aladdin agreed to help.

The old man took Aladdin and Abu to the Cave of Wonders – the same cave where Gazeem disappeared. He wanted Aladdin to retrieve a magical item for him. "Who disturbs my slumber?" the tiger head entrance roared.

"It is I, Aladdin," came the reply.

"Proceed," the tiger thundered. "Touch nothing but the lamp!"

Aladdin and Abu carefully entered the cave. Before long, they entered a huge treasure chamber. A magic carpet appeared and playfully tugged at Abu's tail, then hid behind a pile of gold. "Maybe you can help us," Aladdin said to the carpet. "We're trying to find this lamp."

The carpet led Aladdin and Abu to a lake deep in the cave. At its centre was a huge altar made from rocks, with a lamp sitting on top. He carefully approached it, wondering what all the fuss was about – it didn't look that impressive.

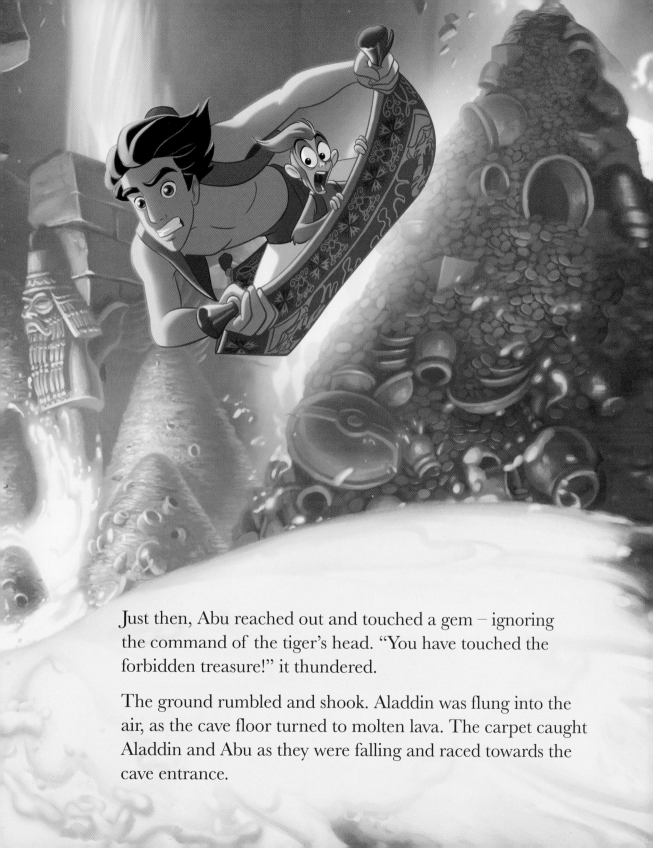

Just then, Abu reached out and touched a gem – ignoring
the command of the tiger's head. "You have touched the
forbidden treasure!" it thundered.

The ground rumbled and shook. Aladdin was flung into the
air, as the cave floor turned to molten lava. The carpet caught
Aladdin and Abu as they were falling and raced towards the
cave entrance.

As they were about to escape, Aladdin fell from the
carpet. He frantically grasped for something to hold
on to, as he begged the old man for help. "First, give
me the lamp!" cried the old man. Aladdin handed
it over and watched as the old man snatched it from
him and fled without helping. Along with Abu,
Aladdin fell to the bottom of the cavern
and towards the hot molten lava.

Outside the cave, it turned out that the old man was actually Jafar in disguise. He was happy to have finally got the lamp. Jafar reached inside his cloak... the lamp had gone and the sorcerer howled with rage!

Back in the cave, which had turned back into stone, Aladdin and Abu had been rescued by the Magic Carpet. Abu still had the lamp, too!

Aladdin rubbed the lamp to get a better look. Suddenly, sparks flew, smoke swirled and – POOF – a genie appeared! "So what'll it be, Master?" the Genie asked. He explained that Aladdin could have three wishes. Aladdin didn't know what to wish for.

The Genie explained he was the best friend Aladdin could ask for. He could give him riches, the most magnificent food and strength beyond words! But there were limitations to the wishes. "Limitations?" asked Aladdin, who glanced at Abu and added, "He probably can't even get us out of this cave."

"Excuse me?" asked the Genie.

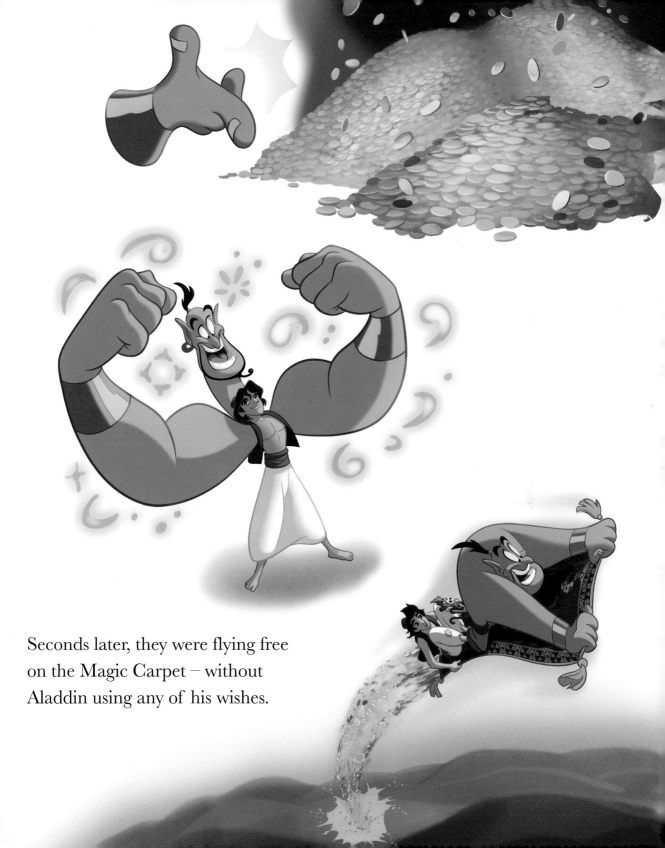

Seconds later, they were flying free
on the Magic Carpet – without
Aladdin using any of his wishes.

Meanwhile, Jasmine was angry with Jafar. She believed
he had got rid of Aladdin forever. Jafar apologised, but
Jasmine would not accept his apology. "At least some good
will come of my being forced to marry," she said. "When I
am queen, I will have the power to get rid of you!"

Safely out of the cave, Aladdin thought about his first wish. He wanted to be with Jasmine. "Genie, I wish for you to make me a prince."

The Genie looked at Aladdin's size and build. He measured here…

… and there. And then, with a wave of his big blue hands…

… presto! The Genie had dressed Aladdin in clothes fit
for a prince. "Hang on to your turban kid!" the Genie
announced. "We're going to make you a star!"

In the blink of an eye, Aladdin found himself riding into Agrabah in a spectacular parade of acrobats, dancers and sword twirlers, along with a large collection of animals – including Abu, who the Genie had changed into an elephant.

Arriving at the palace, Aladdin – calling himself
Prince Ali Ababwa – asked for Jasmine's hand in
marriage. The Sultan was delighted a prince of such
quality wanted to marry his daughter. Jasmine, who
did not recognise Aladdin, was far from impressed.
She wasn't a prize to be won.

Wanting to show Jasmine he wasn't as arrogant as he had appeared, Aladdin, still disguised as Prince Ali Ababwa, visited her that night. "Leave me alone!" said Jasmine, when she saw him on her balcony. She had little interest in a stuck-up prince.

"Please give me a chance," replied Aladdin, who offered her a ride with him on the Magic Carpet.

Excited to go on the Magic Carpet, she happily accepted. As they flew together across deserts, mountains, seas and cities, Jasmine realised that Prince Ali was actually the boy from the market. By the time Aladdin had taken her back to the palace, it was clear the pair were deeply in love with each other.

For the first time in his life, things were starting to go right for Aladdin.

Things quickly went wrong again when the palace guards captured him, with orders from Jafar to throw Aladdin into the sea.

With a ball chained to his legs, Aladdin sank to the bottom of
the sea with the lamp landing nearby. He struggled to reach
the lamp and was quickly running out of air, but he soon
bumped into the lamp. The Genie appeared and used one
of Aladdin's wishes to rescue him. "Don't scare me like that,
kid," said the Genie, as he unchained Aladdin.

At the palace, Jafar had hypnotised the Sultan again. Turning to Jasmine, the Sultan said, "You will wed Jafar."

Just then, Aladdin arrived and revealed Jafar as an evil sorcerer. Jafar caught sight of Aladdin's lamp and realised he was Prince Ali. The villain then escaped, vanishing into thin air.

Not long after, Jafar's parrot, Iago, lured Aladdin outside by copying Jasmine's voice. When Aladdin went to look for her, Iago stole the lamp and gave it to Jafar.

After Jafar rubbed the lamp, he told the Genie his first command.
"I wish to rule on high as sultan!"

The Genie had to obey. He transformed Jafar into the sultan, then lifted the palace into the air. "Genie!" cried Aladdin. "No!"

"Sorry, kid," replied the Genie. "I've got a new master now."

Jafar made his second wish – to be the most powerful sorcerer in the world. Then, he used his new power to send Aladdin and Abu somewhere very cold and far, far away.

Aladdin and Abu huddled together in the snow. "Somehow, I've got to go back and set things right," said Aladdin. Fortunately, it wasn't just Abu who had been sent away with Aladdin, but the Magic Carpet, too! There was still a chance to save Jasmine and stop Jafar's evil plans. "Back to Agrabah!" cried Aladdin.

At the palace, Jafar had strung the Sultan up like a puppet and made Jasmine his slave. He was enjoying his power so much, he didn't notice Aladdin had returned. Jasmine had seen him, however, and tried to distract Jafar so Aladdin could take back the lamp and save everyone. Unfortunately, the sorcerer caught Aladdin's reflection in the princess's tiara.

Jafar swiftly used his magic to imprison
Jasmine in a giant hourglass and turn
Abu into a toy.

Then he trapped Aladdin behind a wall of swords! But, the boy was ready to improvise like he had always done on the streets of Agrabah, and an idea came to him.

"The Genie has more power than you'll
ever have!" Aladdin taunted Jafar.

Infuriated, Jafar used his final wish.
"I wish to be an all-powerful genie!"

Jafar was instantly transformed into a genie. But he had forgotten that a genie is doomed to live in a lamp and obey a master's wishes.

Aladdin picked up Jafar's lamp – and the wicked sorcerer was imprisoned inside it for all time. Genie then threw the lamp deep into the desert.

As a reward for Aladdin's bravery, the Sultan changed the law so
Jasmine could marry whoever she wanted.

Aladdin used his third wish to free the Genie, who couldn't wait
to explore the world. Aladdin and the Genie hugged goodbye, but
they knew they would be friends forever.

THE END

COLLECT THEM ALL!

With 12 more exciting titles to choose from, you'll want to complete your Storytime Collection!

Will Bambi learn the value of friendship?

Will Belle be able to break the curse?

Will Dory finally find her parents?

How far will a father go for his son?

Will Simba ever become king?

Can Anna and Elsa stop an eternal winter?

Will Mowgli defeat Shere Khan?

Will the Incredibles save the day?

Will Ariel be able to find her prince in time?

Can Moana restore the heart of Te Fiti?

Will Maleficent's curse come true?

Will Rapunzel learn who she truly is?

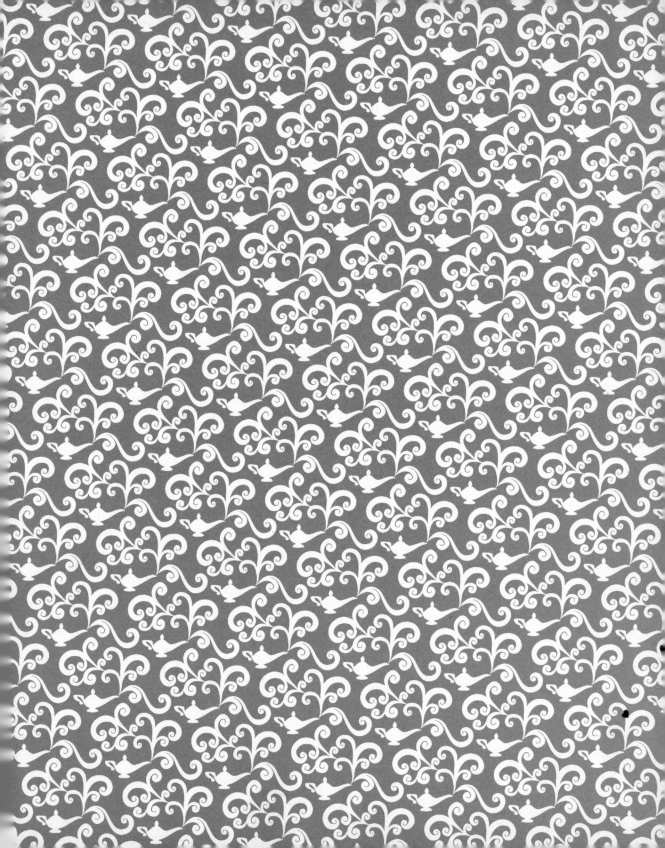